Finding a Friend in the Forest

A True Story

Written and Illustrated by
Dean Bennett

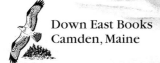

Down East Books
Camden, Maine

Design by Lindy Gifford

Printed in China by Oceanic Graphic Printing Productions Ltd.

5   4   3   2   1

ISBN 0-89272-662-8

Library of Congress Control Number 2005927183

Down East Books
P.O. Box 679
Camden, ME 04843

A division of Down East Enterprise, publishers of *Down East* magazine,
www.downeast.com

To request a book catalog or place an order, visit www.downeastbooks.com,
or call 800-685-7962.

Many people contributed to the development of this book.
I especially thank Regina Webster and John Richardson,
whose deep love for Jasper goes beyond words. Their desire
to have his story told made this book possible. I also thank
Mark Melnicove, who worked with me on an earlier, unpub-
lished piece with many of the same subjects but a different
story line. Mark taught me a lot about writing children's
books. I thank, too, Chris Cornell, my editor, for his help
and encouragement, and my wife, Sheila, who is a constant
source of support and advice. Finally, I was privileged to
know Jasper, and it is to him that I owe the inspiration for
this book.

On a cold, snowy day in the middle of winter, Jasper the beagle and his owners, Reggie and her husband, John, move to their new home—a sporting camp deep in the woods of northern Maine. Here guests will soon come to fish through the thick ice on the big lake in front of the cabin.

Jasper likes to hunt and chase Snowshoe Hare,
who lives in the thick woods around the camp.
But Jasper is getting old, and he can't hear John
and Reggie calling him to come home. John puts
a bell on him so they will know where he is.

Jasper's first visitor is Red Fox, who soon learns that Jasper is slower than he is. One day, Reggie sees Red Fox trot up so close to Jasper that he just can't help but chase this animal with the big, long tail. Around and around a large pine stump they go. Then, suddenly, Red Fox jumps up on the stump and sits down to watch Jasper running circles around him. Reggie decides that Red Fox likes to tease Jasper.

Another day, Jasper is walking toward his cabin when a dark shadow crosses his snowy path. Raven glides in and lands. The big, black bird struts around as if Jasper's yard belongs to him. Raven seems to be everywhere, keeping his eye out for anything to eat. Jasper barks and barks, but try as he may, he just can't scare off the fearless bird.

Jasper likes the taste of fish, and he often goes down onto the frozen lake to check for any scraps he might find around the fishing holes that camp guests have cut through the ice. One late afternoon, just as Jasper is beginning to eat a delicious frozen fish he has found, Raven swoops down and snatches it right out of Jasper's mouth. Raven is someone to watch out for!

This winter, fierce winds roar across the lake's icy surface, and deep drifts of snow pile up like whipped cream around the cabin. At night, the eerie yips and wails of Coyote break the stillness. One evening Jasper sees Coyote slinking in the woods near the back of the camp. The grayish animal stops and stares at the beagle. Jasper gets the feeling that he should stay away from Coyote.

Spring brings warming days, and the ice on the lake disappears.
John puts out the dock and launches a big boat. Guests come for
spring fishing, and Jasper discovers the frogs that live along the
lakeshore. One morning he is so busy trying to catch these
quick jumpers that he doesn't see Moose standing at the water's
edge. The great animal snorts and stamps its hoof only a few feet
from Jasper's nose. Moose is not going to be friendly, either.

Once a week, Jasper goes with John and Reggie in the boat to get groceries. Coming back one day, they see a deer in their front yard. Right away Reggie senses that something is wrong. The small deer stands motionless, like a lawn ornament, as John docks the boat. Jasper feels John's hand around his collar as the three of them move quietly up the camp path toward the scraggly-looking deer. It still doesn't move.

The small doe is thin and weak. Reggie looks down into the deer's face. It's sweet, with long, curling eyelashes, and she can't help but smile broadly. Without thinking, she whispers, "Hi, Sweetie." Reggie holds out a cracker, and when the deer takes a step forward, she sees the animal's injured hind leg. Reggie places the cracker on the ground and steps back. Sweetie stretches her neck out, sniffs, and in a hungry gulp the cracker disappears.

Sweetie begins to show up regularly to feed on the lawn in the camp yard, which is now a bright green, light-filled opening in a dark, tangled forest of spruce and fir. Jasper doesn't welcome Sweetie, and John has to tell him not to chase her. So when Sweetie trots onto the lawn, the beagle parades back and forth in front of her, as if to guard every blade of grass. Sweetie keeps her distance.

The dry heat of summer creeps into the surrounding forest, and the woods hum with insects. Trout swim away from the shoreline to find cool water in the deeper parts of the lake. Sweetie's strength returns, and her hind leg heals, although she still limps. "She runs like a cow," John jokes. As the days pass, Jasper and Sweetie seem to accept each other, and sometimes the deer follows the beagle around the camp yard. Reggie and John wonder if Jasper is finding a friend.

October brings cold weather and a covering of
snow. The lake freezes over, and winter comes
once again. Jasper finds Bobcat's tracks behind
the camp, and at night Coyote howls. John and
Reggie worry that Sweetie, in deep snow with
her weak leg, might be in danger from these
predators.

One cold winter's day, when Jasper is down on the ice, Sweetie suddenly bounds out of the woods toward him with Coyote right behind her. When she gets close, Jasper recognizes her. Then he sees Coyote and begins to growl and bark. Coyote turns and runs back into the woods. He will have to go hungry a while longer.

Sweetie now stays close to the camp. Jasper's scent keeps
Coyote away. Sometimes John and Reggie see the deer sleeping
under their cabin. With the coming of spring, Sweetie often goes
back into the woods. She stays away longer and longer, until one
day she doesn't return. Every now and then, Reggie sees Jasper
looking for Sweetie in her sleeping place under the cabin.
"I think Jasper misses Sweetie," Reggie tells John. So do they.

One evening, as summer approaches, Reggie and John are surprised and happy when they look out a window of their cabin and see Sweetie come out of the woods. But she is not alone; she is followed by three spotted fawns. Jasper sees the deer, too, and quickly starts toward them. Reggie and John watch in silence, wondering what Sweetie will do. They know how protective a doe can be with her fawns.

Jasper stops and looks at the four deer.
Sweetie steps between her fawns and
him. For a moment, she doesn't move.
Then she slowly walks toward Jasper until
she is very close. Her head drops down,
and she touches her nose to Jasper's. The
two friends have found each other again.

Sweetie came back to the sporting camp for another
fourteen years, and each year she brought new fawns
with her—sometimes triplets. Jasper lived a very
long life for a dog, more than eighteen years, and saw
his yard filled with as many as twelve deer at a time.
The setting for this book is in Maine's Allagash
Wilderness Waterway, which—like most wild places
and wild creatures—needs friends, too.